Cam's teacher is in big trouble!

Ms. Benson walked through the room. She looked at the children's work and smiled. Then the door opened. Two police officers walked in. One was very tall, and one was not so tall and had a short beard.

Ms. Benson hurried to the front of the room.

"I'm Officer Oppen," said the not-so-tall officer. He showed her a slip of paper and asked, "Is this your car's license-plate number?"

Ms. Benson nodded.

"Did you drive your car to school this morning?"

"Yes," Ms. Benson said.

"You left the scene of an accident," the tall officer told her.

"No I didn't," Ms. Benson said quickly. "There must be some mistake."

"Please," the officer with the short beard said. "You'll have to come with us."

CAM JANSEN

The First Day of
School Mystery

CAM JANSEN

CASE #22

The First Day of School Mystery

David A. Adler
Illustrated by Susanna Natti

PUFFIN BOOKS
An Imprint of Penguin Group (USA) Inc.

PUFFIN BOOKS
Published by the Penguin Group
Penguin Young Readers Group, 345 Hudson Street, New York, New York 10014, U.S.A.
Penguin Group (Canada), 90 Eglinton Avenue East, Suite 700, Toronto, Ontario, Canada M4P 2Y3
(a division of Pearson Penguin Canada Inc.)
Penguin Books Ltd, 80 Strand, London WC2R 0RL, England
Penguin Ireland, 25 St Stephen's Green, Dublin 2, Ireland (a division of Penguin Books Ltd)
Penguin Group (Australia), 250 Camberwell Road, Camberwell, Victoria 3124, Australia
(a division of Pearson Australia Group Pty Ltd)
Penguin Books India Pvt Ltd, 11 Community Centre,
Panchsheel Park, New Delhi - 110 017, India
Penguin Group (NZ), 67 Apollo Drive, Rosedale, North Shore 0632, New Zealand
(a division of Pearson New Zealand Ltd)
Penguin Books (South Africa) (Pty) Ltd, 24 Sturdee Avenue,
Rosebank, Johannesburg 2196, South Africa

Registered Offices: Penguin Books Ltd, 80 Strand, London WC2R 0RL, England

First published in the United States of America by Viking,
a division of Penguin Putnam Books for Young Readers, 2002
Published by Puffin Books, a division of Penguin Young Readers Group, 2003, 2005
This edition published by Puffin Books, a division of Penguin Young Readers Group, 2011

21 23 25 27 29 30 28 26 24 22

THE LIBRARY OF CONGRESS HAS CATALOGED THE VIKING EDITION AS FOLLOWS:
Adler, David A.
Cam Jansen and the first day of school mystery / David A. Adler ;
illustrated by Susanna Natti.
p. cm.—(A Cam Jansen adventure ; 22)
Summary: On her first day of fifth grade, Cam Jansen uses her photographic memory
to help the police find a car thief.
Includes a memory game.
ISBN: 0-670-03575-0 (hardcover)
[1. First day of school—Fiction. 2. Schools—Fiction. 3. Memory—Fiction.
4. Mystery and detective stories.]
I. Title.
PZ7.A2615 Caaef 2002
[Fic]—dc21   01-056803

Puffin Books ISBN 978-0-14-240326-6

Printed in the United States of America

RL: 2.0

For my children,
Michael, Deborah, Eddie, and Eitan.
—D.A.

To Emma and Michael.
—S.N.

CHAPTER ONE

"I give up!" Mrs. Lane said. "We'll *never* get to school!"

Mrs. Lane was driving a school bus. It was stuck in traffic.

"Never get to school!" a small boy said, and started to cry. "Never get to school!" he said again. "How will I learn to read? How will I learn to write?"

"Don't worry," Cam Jansen told the boy, and smiled. "We'll get to school."

Cam and her friend Eric Shelton sat near the front of the bus, right behind the boy. Eric asked the boy his name.

"Tommy," the boy said. "I'm in kinder-garten."

"Well, Tommy-in-Kindergarten," Eric said softly, "Mrs. Lane always complains about the traffic, and we always get to school."

"This time it's different," Mrs. Lane said. "This time the cars are not moving at all."

Cam looked out the window. There was a long line of cars ahead. None of them were

moving. People were standing outside their cars, trying to see what was wrong. There was also a long line of cars behind the bus.

Mrs. Lane banged on the horn.

Honk! Honk!

A man in a car just ahead threw up his hands. There was nothing he could do.

Honk! Honk!

Other people banged on their horns. But none of the cars moved.

"My teacher's name is Mr. Gale," Tommy-in-Kindergarten said. "I know because the principal sent a letter."

"A letter!" Eric said. "Oh, no! I don't remember our teacher's name. I don't remember our room number." Eric searched in his backpack. "I can't find Dr. Prell's letter."

"Don't worry," Cam told him. "We're in the same class and I remember."

Cam closed her eyes and said, "*Click!*"

Cam always says "*Click!*" when she wants to remember something. "My mind is like a camera," Cam says, "and cameras go *Click!*"

Cam remembers just about everything. It's as if she has a mental camera and photographs in her head of whatever she's seen.

Mrs. Lane banged on the horn again.

Honk! Honk!

The cars ahead still didn't move.

Cam's real name is Jennifer. But when people found out about her amazing memory they started calling her "The Camera." Soon "The Camera" became just "Cam."

"'Dear Jennifer Jansen,'" Cam said with her eyes still closed. "'Welcome to the fifth grade.'"

"Here it is," Eric said. "I found the letter."

Cam kept reading from the picture of the letter she had in her head.

"'Your teacher this year will be Ms. Benson in Room 118. School begins at 8:30 A.M., Wednesday, September 6. Please bring

a pencil, pen, notebook, and an eagerness to learn. With best wishes for a great school year, Dr. Jane Prell, principal.'"

"You got every word right," Eric said.

Cam smiled. She opened her eyes.

"And I'm right, too," Mrs. Lane told the children. She turned the key and shut off the bus. "If the cars ahead don't move, we'll never get to school."

Mrs. Lane took a small telephone from her pocket. Some papers fell out. She pressed the buttons on the telephone and waited.

"Dr. Prell," she said. "This is Sally Lane, the bus driver. I'm stuck on Franklin Street, three blocks from the school. . . . Oh, my. That's terrible. . . . Of course . . . Yes, I'll get the children ready."

CHAPTER TWO

Mrs. Lane put the telephone in her pocket. She turned and spoke to the children. "Get your books and things together. A teacher will be here in a few minutes. He'll walk with you to school."

Cam and Eric looked out the window and waited. They saw Mr. Day, the gym teacher, walking toward them. When he reached the bus, he blew his whistle.

Trill! Trill!

"Let's go," he shouted. "Line up out here."

Children hurried down the aisle and off

the bus. They stood behind Mr. Day.

"Get in a straight double line," he shouted. "Hold hands."

Cam and Eric waited until the last children were off the bus before leaving their seats. When Cam passed Mrs. Lane she picked up some papers.

"Are these yours?" Cam asked.

"Oh yes. Thank you," Mrs. Lane said. "This yellow one is a message from my boss. I'm glad you found it. And this pink one is my dry-cleaning ticket. I'm just losing everything!"

Cam and Eric got off the bus and went to the back of the line.

"Hold hands!" Mr. Day told them.

Cam and Eric held hands.

"I feel like I'm in kindergarten," Eric said.

"I *am* in kindergarten," Tommy-in-Kindergarten said.

"Quiet in the back!" Mr. Day shouted.

The children walked past people stuck in their cars. Some were resting or reading. Others were talking on small telephones. Some people smiled and waved to the children.

"Look," Eric whispered. "Police cars! Maybe there was an accident."

Cam and Eric kept walking. Then they saw a large tree. When they walked past the tree they saw the front end of a small green car. It had crashed into the tree.

"I hope no one was hurt," Eric said.

"Quiet in the back!" Mr. Day shouted.

Cam and Eric walked quietly. Then, when

they were close to the car, Cam whispered, "Stop."

Mr. Day and the other children kept walking. Cam waited until the others were a bit ahead. Then she whispered, "The car doesn't look so bad, and there's no ambulance, so maybe no one was hurt."

Police officers were standing by their cars, talking. Cam looked at the green car. She blinked her eyes and said, *"Click!"*

Cam and Eric got close to the car and looked in.

"There are papers on the front seat, a white one and a pink one," Cam told Eric. "There's a pair of sneakers on the floor and a tennis racket in the back."

Cam blinked her eyes again and said, "*Click!*"

"Get away from there," a tall police officer told Cam and Eric.

"Let's go," Mr. Day called to them.

Cam and Eric ran to the line. They quietly followed Mr. Day and the other children into the school. They went to Room 118, opened the door, and met their new teacher, Ms. Benson.

CHAPTER THREE

"You must be Jennifer," Ms. Benson said to Cam. "And you must be Eric. Your seats are in the back."

"How does she know our names?" Eric whispered.

"She has a class list. All teachers do," Cam told him. "Everyone else is here, so who else could we be?"

Cam and Eric looked at the children already sitting at their desks. Lots of their friends and classmates from fourth grade were in Ms. Benson's class. They were busy copying a list of classroom rules from the chalkboard.

In the front of each desk, right in the middle, was a neatly written name tag. Cam and Eric found their name tags. Their desks were next to each other. They sat down and began to copy Ms. Benson's classroom rules.

Ms. Benson walked through the room. She looked at the children's work and smiled. Then the door opened. Two police officers walked in. One was very tall, and one was not so tall and had a short beard.

"I remember the tall policeman," Cam whispered to Eric. "He told us to get away from the car."

Ms. Benson hurried to the front of the room.

"I'm Officer Oppen," said the not-so-tall officer. He showed her a slip of paper and asked, "Is this your car's license-plate number?"

Ms. Benson nodded.

"Did you drive your car to school this morning?"

"Yes," Ms. Benson said.

"You left the scene of an accident," the tall officer told her.

"No I didn't," Ms. Benson said quickly. "There must be some mistake."

"Please," the officer with the short beard said. "You'll have to come with us."

Ms. Benson turned to the class. "Sit quietly," she said. Then she left the room with the tall officer on one side and the shorter one on the other.

The children did *not* sit quietly.

Danny got up. He put his hands on his hips and said in a high squeaky voice, "*There must be some mistake!*"

Danny lowered his voice, pointed, and said, "*You'll have to come with us.*"

He laughed. "My mother told *me* not to get in trouble. Well, I didn't. My teacher did! She got arrested!"

CHAPTER FOUR

"We saw her car," Eric said. "It's green and it crashed right into a tree just one block from here. That's why Cam and I were late. Our bus was stuck in traffic."

"They should have put handcuffs on her," Danny said. "They should have told her she has the right to remain silent."

Cam closed her eyes. She said, "*Click!*" She looked at the picture she had in her head of the small green car.

Dr. Prell came in. Danny quickly sat down.

Cam opened her eyes.

"There are books in the back," Dr. Prell told the class. "Please find something to read. There will be a teacher here soon."

Dr. Prell watched as children went to the classroom library and selected books. Cam chose a mystery. Eric took a biography.

Cam sat in her seat. She opened the mystery, but she kept thinking about Ms. Benson and the small green car.

"Here I am," Mr. Day said as he walked into the room.

"I hope Ms. Benson will be back soon," Dr. Prell told him. "The children are reading," she said, and left the room.

Mr. Day slowly walked by the children's desks. He looked at what they were reading.

Cam closed her eyes again and said, "*Click!*" She looked again at the picture she had in her head of the green car that crashed into the tree.

"Your eyes are closed. You're not reading," Mr. Day said.

Cam opened her eyes. Mr. Day was standing right by her desk.

"You should be reading," Mr. Day told her.

Cam looked at the mystery. Then, when Mr. Day walked away, she closed her eyes again and looked at the picture of the green car and the tree.

"That's it!" Cam called out. "Ms. Benson was telling the truth. I can prove it!"

"It's you again," Mr. Day said. "You

shouldn't be calling out. You should be reading."

"But this is important," Cam told him. "I have to speak with Dr. Prell."

"Just do what you're told," Mr. Day said. "Sit quietly and read."

Cam looked at her mystery again. Just then a small folded piece of paper landed in the middle of the book. Cam opened it.

It was from Eric. *Are you sure?* was written on the note.

Yes! Cam added to the note. Then she folded it and tossed it to Eric.

"Now you're sending notes!" Mr. Day shouted. He hurried to Eric. "Give me that," he said.

"Come with me," Mr. Day told Cam.

Cam followed him to the front of the room.

"Now *I'm* sending a note," he said as he wrote. He clipped Cam and Eric's note to his and said, "Take this to Dr. Prell."

Cam took the notes and left the room. Once she was in the hall, she smiled. She was going to see Dr. Prell. That was just what she wanted to do.

CHAPTER FIVE

"I'm here to see Dr. Prell," Cam told Mrs. Wayne, the principal's secretary. Cam gave her the note.

"Do you still click? Do you still have a photographic memory?" Mrs. Wayne asked.

"Yes," Cam answered.

"Amazing, just amazing," Mrs. Wayne said as she knocked on the door to Dr. Prell's office.

"Yes?" Dr. Prell called.

Mrs. Wayne opened the office door. She

gave Dr. Prell the note and said, "It's the clicking girl."

Dr. Prell read the note. Then she waved for Cam to come in. "Cam," she said. "I'm surprised at you. You're in trouble on the very first day of school."

"I can prove Ms. Benson didn't crash her car into that tree."

"You can?" Dr. Prell asked.

"I was in Mrs. Lane's bus," Cam said. "I walked past the accident, and I remember that the car was facing the wrong way."

"The wrong way?"

"Yes," Cam said. "It was going *away* from school when it crashed into the tree. This morning, when Ms. Benson came here, she would have been driving *toward* the school."

"The car was facing away from school? Are you sure?" Dr. Prell asked. But before Cam could answer, Dr. Prell said, "Of course you're sure. You're Cam Jansen."

Dr. Prell picked up the telephone and

called the police. She asked for Officer Oppen. Then she gave Cam the telephone receiver.

"Yes?" the police officer on the other end of the line asked.

Cam told him why she was sure Ms. Benson hadn't crashed her car into the tree.

"I think you're right," the officer said. "We spoke with Ms. Benson and some of the other teachers. She was in her classroom at the time of the accident. Someone must have stolen her car from the school parking lot. The thief was the one who left the scene of the accident."

"Someone stole Ms. Benson's car!" Cam said. "Who did it?"

"*That's* still a mystery," the police officer said, "and we plan to solve it."

CHAPTER SIX

Cam put down the telephone. "After Ms. Benson came to school and parked her car, it was stolen," she told Dr. Prell.

"From our parking lot?" Dr. Prell asked.

Cam nodded.

Dr. Prell turned. She looked through her window at the cars parked outside and said, "Whoever stole Ms. Benson's car probably saw her park it. He knew she's a teacher and wouldn't come back until school was over. There would be plenty of time before Ms. Benson would notice her car was missing. By then he could be a long way from here."

"You said, '*He* knew she's a teacher,' and 'By then *he* could be a long way from here.' Do you know the thief is a man?"

"No," Dr. Prell admitted. "I don't know that."

"Women steal, too."

"You're right," Dr. Prell said.

"And the thief *would* be a long way from here," Cam said, "if he or she hadn't crashed into that tree."

Cam thought for a moment. Then she said, "The thief must have left fingerprints on the steering wheel. And maybe someone saw the thief get out of the car."

Dr. Prell turned from the window. "What did the police officer say?" she asked.

"He said this is a mystery."

Dr. Prell nodded. "The police know all about fingerprints and witnesses. Let them look for the thief."

"But—" Cam started.

Dr. Prell stopped her. "You're a smart girl," she said. "I know you like to solve mysteries, but I think you'll have to leave this one to the police."

Cam nodded.

"You should go back to class now," Dr. Prell told her.

Cam started toward the door.

"And Cam," Dr. Prell said, "Ms. Benson is a *very* good teacher. I'm sure you and your class will have a great year."

Dr. Prell wrote a note to Mr. Day and gave it to Cam.

Cam left the principal's office.

"*Click! Click!*" Mrs. Wayne said, and laughed as Cam walked past.

Cam smiled and said, "*Click! Click!*"

When Cam got back to class, the children were all standing by their desks. Their arms were raised high above their heads.

Cam gave Mr. Day the note. He looked at it. Then he told Cam, "Go stand by your seat. Lift up your arms and stretch. Exercise will help you think."

Cam raised her arms above her head.

"Arms out," Mr. Day said.

He stretched his arms in front of him. Cam and the others in her class did, too.

"Now, right arm up, left to the side," Mr. Day said.

Mr. Day demonstrated, and the children followed his example.

"Left knees up and hop."

The children raised their left knees and hopped.

A few children banged into their desks. Two boys in Cam's row fell.

The door opened. Ms. Benson came in. She looked at the hopping children. Then she looked at Mr. Day.

"This exercise will help them think," he told her.

The children kept hopping, knocking into their desks, and falling.

Ms. Benson smiled. "Rabbits and kangaroos must be great thinkers," she said.

"Rabbits and kangaroos?" Mr. Day asked.

"They hop a lot," Ms. Benson explained.

"Oh," Mr. Day said. He stopped hopping. He told the children to be seated. Ms. Benson thanked him for watching her class, and he left.

Ms. Benson stood in front of the class. "This has been a strange first day of school," she said. "I didn't plan to be in the police station this morning. I planned to teach. And that's what I'm going to do."

Ms. Benson asked the children to take out their math notebooks. She was about to teach them how to multiply fractions.

You plan to teach, Cam thought, *and I plan to solve this mystery. I plan to find out who stole your car.*

CHAPTER SEVEN

Ms. Benson drew large circles on the board. She called them "pies" and drew slices in them. She wrote lots of numbers and fractions on the board. She talked on and on about multiplication and fractions.

Cam's classmates listened to Ms. Benson. When she put some problems on the board, they did them. Cam didn't. She kept thinking about Ms. Benson's car.

Rrrr!

The school bell rang.

"Oh, my," Ms. Benson said. "I just started teaching, and it's already time for lunch."

The children closed their books and hurried out of the room.

"Jennifer," Ms. Benson called to Cam. "Please wait."

Cam and Eric stopped by Ms. Benson's desk.

"I know I wasn't listening to the lesson," Cam told Ms. Benson. "But I was thinking about your car. There must be some way to find out who stole it."

"That's a job for the police," Ms. Benson said.

"Cam is really good at solving mysteries," Eric said.

"Cam? Who's Cam?" Ms. Benson asked.

Eric explained to her about Cam's amazing memory. "And we saw your car this morning," Eric said. "Maybe Cam will remember something that will help the police."

Ms. Benson smiled. "I don't think the police need your help," she said. "I think you should go to lunch. And when you get back, pay attention to the lesson."

Cam and Eric went to the cafeteria. They sat at a table by the window and opened their lunch bags.

"Hey," Danny, called to Cam from the next table. "Did Benson yell at you? Are you in trouble for not doing the math?"

"I'm not in trouble," Cam answered.

"Oh yes you are," Danny said. "That Benson is tough."

"I think she's nice," Janet Teller said.

Cam unwrapped her sandwich. While she and Eric ate their lunches, they talked with their friends about the summer and Ms. Benson.

Eric pushed a straw into his drink container and grabbed it. Juice squirted out of the straw and onto his shirt.

"Yikes!" Eric said. "Look what I did!"

"You should be more careful," Janet said.

After lunch, the children returned to class, and Ms. Benson started a geography lesson.

"What's the world's most important food?" she asked.

"Cotton candy," Danny called out.

"Please, raise your hand," Ms. Benson told him.

"Milk is important," Janet said when Ms. Benson called on her.

"Yes. That's true," Ms. Benson said. "But for more than half the people of the world, rice is their most important food."

Cam tried to pay attention to the lesson, but she kept thinking about Ms. Benson's car.

"And other than water," Ms. Benson said, "people have more coffee than any other drink."

"More than soda? More than juice?" Danny asked.

Juice, Cam thought. She looked at Eric. There was a stain where juice had spilled on his shirt.

I wonder, Cam thought.

Cam closed her eyes. She said, "*Click!*" and looked at a picture she had in her head.

"I just remembered something," Cam called out, and opened her eyes. "Ms. Benson, I just remembered something I saw in your car."

CHAPTER EIGHT

"Cam said, '*Click!*'" Danny called out, and got up. "Hey, I'm a camera," he said, and blinked his eyes a few times. "*Click! Click! Click!*"

Janet turned to Danny. "Don't make fun of Cam," she told him.

"What did you remember?" the other children asked Cam.

"Please, sit down," Ms. Benson told Danny. "And if you want to say something to me or to the class, please raise your hand."

Cam raised her hand.

"Do you want to say something?" Ms. Benson asked Cam.

"Yes," Cam answered. "When you talked about drinks, I remembered that Eric spilled his drink. Then I thought about cleaning his shirt and I wanted to ask you if you brought some clothing to the cleaners this morning."

"That's a strange question."

"There's a cleaners near the school," Cam said. "Mrs. Lane, our bus driver, goes to it. This morning, while she was driving, a cleaning ticket fell out of her pants pocket."

"I didn't go to the cleaners this morning."

"Well," Cam said. "There was a pink piece of paper on the front seat of your car. I think it's a cleaning ticket."

"I saw it, too," Eric called out.

"It's not mine," Ms. Benson said. She thought for a moment. "And do you know what's on a cleaning ticket?" she said as she went to her closet. "A name."

Ms. Benson opened her closet. She took out a small telephone, and pressed some buttons.

"Hello Officer Oppen," she said. "This is Margie Benson."

"Margie," Danny whispered. "Our teacher's name is Margie."

"There may be a cleaning ticket in my car," Ms. Benson said, "but it isn't mine. It might be the thief's. If it is, the thief's name will be on the ticket."

Ms. Benson listened. Then she thanked Officer Oppen and said good-bye.

"This is exciting," she said, and smiled at Cam.

Ms. Benson returned the telephone to her closet. "Well," she said to the class. "Let's continue the lesson."

Ms. Benson went to the bulletin board on the side wall. "Most of the world's rice grows in Asia," she said. She pointed to the map of the world and asked, "Who can find Asia?"

"Who lost it?" Danny asked.

Ms. Benson glared at Danny. Then she looked at the children who had raised their hands. She called on Eric and asked him to come to the map and find Asia.

He did.

Ms. Benson continued the lesson. She told the children where coffee beans grow. Then she asked them to find those continents on the map.

Cam was no longer listening. She thought about the cleaning ticket and wondered if the police would find the thief.

CHAPTER NINE

Just before the end of the school day, the door to Ms. Benson's classroom opened. Dr. Prell and the police officer with the short beard walked in.

Dr. Prell told Ms. Benson, "Officer Oppen has good news."

Officer Oppen smiled. "We caught the car thief," he told Ms. Benson. "But something still puzzles me. How did you know there was a ticket in the car?"

"She didn't!" Danny shouted, and jumped up. He pointed at Cam. "*She's* the smart one. She has a *Click! Click!* memory."

"That's right. Jennifer Jansen knew about the ticket," Ms. Benson said, and pointed to Cam. "I'm lucky to have smart students." She told Officer Oppen about Cam's amazing memory.

"That cleaning ticket helped to solve the mystery," Officer Oppen told her. "We looked at the name and address on the ticket and we knew who stole the car."

Officer Oppen told Ms. Benson that the thief was at the police station. "He told us he was walking home from the cleaners when he saw you park your car. He told us he was only borrowing it, that he was going to return it before school was out."

Danny called out, "I don't believe him."

Officer Oppen said Ms. Benson's car would have to stay at the police station. Then it would have to be repaired.

Dr. Prell told Ms. Benson, "I can drive you home."

"Well," Officer Oppen said, "that's about it."

Officer Oppen put his hands on his hips and tried to look mean. "Unless there are some other problems here."

When he said that, he looked right at Danny.

Danny was still standing.

Ms. Benson asked Danny, "Do we have any problems here?"

"No," he said, and quickly sat down.

Rrrr!

The school bell rang. It was time to go home.

While the children got ready to leave, Ms. Benson thanked Cam for her help. "I'm glad you're in my class."

Eric was standing next to Cam.

Ms. Benson told Eric, "I'm glad you're in my class, too."

Officer Oppen thanked Cam. "The best defense against crime," he said, "is alert citizens."

"We have to go," Eric said, "or we'll miss our bus."

Cam and Eric hurried out of the room.

"Don't run!" Mr. Day shouted to them from the other end of the hall.

Cam and Eric stopped running.

"There you are," Mrs. Lane said when Cam and Eric got on the bus. "I thought you'd never get here and we'd never get home."

"Never get home!" Tommy-in-Kindergarten said. "How will I eat my dinner! How will I get to sleep!"

"I'm sorry, Tommy," Mrs. Lane said. "I always complain."

"And we always get home in time for dinner," Eric told Tommy-in-Kindergarten. Then Eric turned to Cam and said, "And you always solve mysteries."

"Not *always*," Cam said.

"Well, lots of times," Eric told her. "And I'm *always* happy to help."

Mrs. Lane started to drive off. It was time to ride home after a very exciting first day of school.

A Cam Jansen Memory Game

Take another look at the picture opposite page 1. Study it. Blink your eyes and say *"Click!"* Then turn back to this page and answer these questions. Please, first study the picture, *then* look at the questions.

1. Are Cam and Eric sitting in the seats right behind the bus driver, Mrs. Lane?
2. Where are Mrs. Lane's sunglasses?
3. Is Cam wearing sandals or sneakers?
4. Is Cam wearing a jacket?
5. How many children are wearing hats?
6. Are there any animals in the picture? What kind?